ILLUMINATION PRESENTS

MINIONS

5-Minute STORIES

Little, Brown and Company
New York Boston

Despicable Me: The World's Greatest Villain originally published in 2010 by LB kids
Despicable Me 2: Undercover Super Spies originally published in 2013 by LB kids
Despicable Me 2: Attack of the Evil Minions! originally published in 2013 by Little, Brown and Company
Minions: Dracula's Last Birthday originally published in 2015 by LB kids
Minions Paradise: Phil Saves the Day! originally published in 2016 by LB kids
Despicable Me Minion Made: Mower Minions originally published in 2016 by LB kids

Cover design by Ching N. Chan.

Little, Brown and Company
Hachette Book Group
1290 Avenue of the Americas, New York, NY 10104
Visit us at lbyr.com

First Bindup Edition: March 2022

Little, Brown and Company is a division of Hachette Book Group, Inc. The Little, Brown name and logo are trademarks of Hachette Book Group, Inc.

The publisher is not responsible for websites (or their content) that are not owned by the publisher.

Library of Congress Control Numbers:

Despicable Me: The World's Greatest Villain: 2011287325
Despicable Me 2: Undercover Super Spies: 2013930631
Despicable Me 2: Attack of the Evil Minions!: 2012955439
Minions: Dracula's Last Birthday: 2015930748
Minions Paradise: Phil Saves the Day: 2016288049
Despicable Me Minion Made: Mower Minions: 2016288014

ISBNs: 978-0-316-31831-0 (novelty), 978-0-316-31849-5 (ebook), 978-0-316-36310-5 (ebook), 978-0-316-36320-4 (ebook)

PRINTED IN CHINA

APS

10 9 8 7 6 5 4 3 2

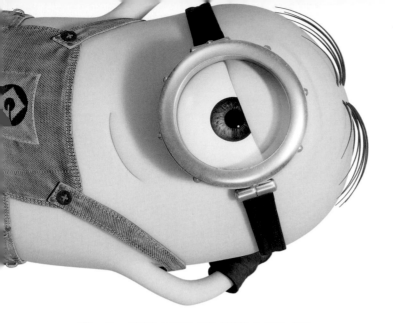

CONTENTS

Despicable Me: The World's Greatest Villain 1

Despicable Me 2: Undercover Super Spies 25

Despicable Me 2: Attack of the Evil Minions! 49

Minions: Dracula's Last Birthday 79

Minions Paradise: Phil Saves the Day! 105

Despicable Me Minion Made: Mower Minions 131

The World's Greatest Villain

Adapted by Kirsten Mayer
Based on the Story by Sergio Pablos
Based on the Screenplay by Cinco Paul and Ken Daurio
Illustrated by Don Cassity, Charlie Grosvenor,
Peter Moehrle, Dave Williams, and Keith Wong

This is Gru.

Gru has a very cool job—he's a professional villain. He has a Freeze Ray, a big black house, and a scary dog named Kyle to prove it.

Some people have basements, or cellars, or just a lot of dirt under their houses. Not Gru. Underneath his big black house, he has a huge secret lair and a secret lab where a mad scientist named Dr. Nefario and an army of little yellow Minions work on Gru's villainous plans.

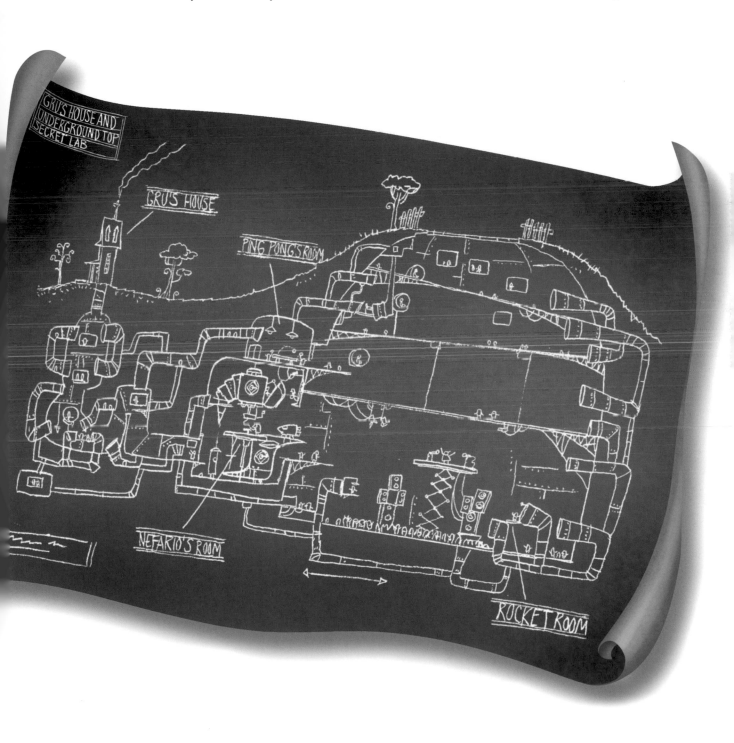

Gru dreams of being the greatest villain in the world. He has behaved badly in the past, popping kids' balloons and freezing customers at the coffee shop so that he could move to the front of the line. But Gru wants to do something BIGGER.

Gru sits with his dog, Kyle, in front of the TV looking for an idea. The news interrupts his show.

"This just in!" shouts the newsman on TV. "The Great Pyramid of Giza has been stolen and replaced by a pyramid-shaped balloon! It's being called the Crime of the Century!"

The phone rings. Gru knows it's his mother.

"Hello, Mom," he says.

"I wanted to congratulate you on stealing the pyramid," she says.
"That *was* you, wasn't it? Or was it a villain who's actually successful?"
Gru knows his mom is just rubbing it in. He sighs and hangs up.

Who is this other villain? Gru wonders. He wishes he had thought of stealing the pyramid first.

Suddenly, Gru has a big idea—an idea for the biggest crime EVER!

He runs down to his secret underground lab to tell Dr. Nefario and the Minions his big plan.

"We are going to find a Shrink Ray! We will then pull off the true Crime of the Century! We are going to steal . . . the MOON!" he tells them.

The Minions all cheer. This is the most villainous idea they have ever heard!

"Once the moon is mine," explains Gru, "the world will give me whatever I want to get it back, and I will be the greatest villain of all time!"

Dr. Nefario isn't so sure about this new plan. They have to find a Shrink Ray and build a rocket to go to the moon. . . . Those things are expensive.

"Hey, Gru," the mad scientist whispers. "I don't see how we can afford this."

Gru just shrugs. He has a plan for that, too.

Gru goes to the Bank of Evil to get a loan. In the lobby, another villain is waiting for a loan, too. Gru doesn't like the look of him. He has a nerdy haircut.

"Hey, I go by the name of Vector," the other guy says. "It's a mathematical term—I'm committing crimes with both direction and magnitude."

Vector shows Gru the Piranha Blaster he invented, but Gru is unimpressed. He doesn't want a friend; he just wants to steal the moon.

But the bank manager won't give him a loan. "There are lots of new villains," he says, "like that young fellow out there named Vector. He just stole the pyramid!"

Gru can't believe his ears. Gru decides to officially make Vector his nemesis.

Since Gru can't afford to buy a Shrink Ray, he does what most villains would do: he *steals* a Shrink Ray. The Minions help him steal it, but just when Gru is about to fly away with his new gadget, he hears a buzzing sound.

BZZZZZT! A laser cuts a hole in the top of Gru's plane! Then a giant claw reaches in and steals the stolen Shrink Ray!

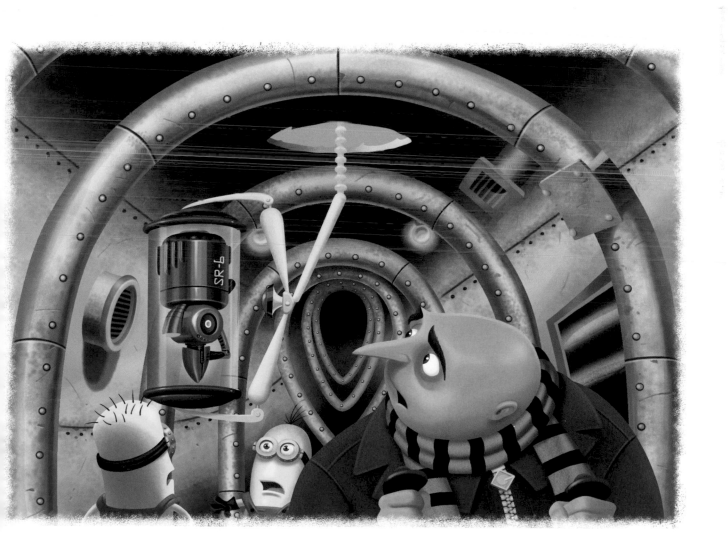

Gru looks out the window—it's Vector!
"Quick, don't let him get away!" Gru shouts.
The Minions fire everything they've got at
Vector's shiny white plane, but Gru's nemesis
easily dodges them.

A mechanical arm emerges from Vector's plane, holding the Shrink Ray aimed at Gru's vehicle.

"Hey, Gru," yells Vector. "Try this one on for size!" MZZZP! A bolt of lightning shoots out of the ray and hits Gru's plane. As his plane shrinks smaller and smaller, Gru begins to plan his revenge.

15

Vector lives in a sleek white house. Gru tries to sneak in and steal back the Shrink Ray, but Vector has too many booby traps.

Giant saws pop out and cut the ropes Gru is climbing. A catapult springs forward and tosses Gru back over the wall. There's even a shark that jumps up to bite him!

Then Gru sees little girls selling cookies! Vector lets them in while he places an order.

Lightbulb! Gru now has a new villainous plan!

A few days later, the girls return to deliver the cookies—but Gru has filled one box with cookie-shaped robots.

Once inside, Gru uses a remote control to operate the Cookie Bots. The robots sprout legs and steal back the Shrink Ray!

Vector quickly realizes the Shrink Ray is gone, and he starts plotting his own revenge. He has heard about Gru's plan to steal the moon. . . . It's pretty good. Vector decides to steal the moon himself.

"Wait until Gru sees my Squid Launcher!" Vector says. "The moon is as good as mine!"

Meanwhile, Gru has already put the Shrink Ray aboard a space rocket. "The plan is simple," he tells himself. "I fly to the moon. I shrink the moon. I grab the moon."

Just as Gru's rocket lifts off, Vector arrives and shoots his Squid Launcher. The slimy squid sticks to the side of the rocket, yanking Vector along into space!

Gru aims the Shrink Ray at the moon. BZZZT! It works! The moon shrinks to the size of a baseball. Gru grabs it, but then his nemesis floats by! Vector surprises Gru and steals the stolen moon.

Before Gru can grab it back, Dr. Nefario puts in a call to Gru. "The Shrink Ray effect is only temporary!" the scientist says. "You can't steal the moon!"

Gru drifts back into his rocket. He smiles out the window at Vector and then blasts back to Earth.

Suddenly, the tiny moon in Vector's hand
begins to grow and grow and grow, until
it is back to full size. Vector is stranded on
the moon!

Gru races home in his rocket and then
runs outside to admire the night sky.

"Good night, Vector," he calls out.
"Until next time!"

UNDERCOVER SUPER SPIES

Adapted by Kirsten Mayer
Illustrated by Arthur Fong & Christophe Lautrette
Based on the Motion Picture Screenplay
Written by Cinco Paul & Ken Daurio

There's a villain on the loose! Someone is using a giant magnetic ship to steal a top secret formula from a top secret laboratory!

And it's *so* top secret that only a top secret group of spies knows about it. The spies also know that to catch a villain, you need the help of another villain....

Or, at least, a former villain.

Gru used to be one of the best super villains in the world! He and his army of Minions even stole the moon!

But then he adopted Margo, Edith, and Agnes and became a dad. Now, instead of stealing landmarks, he makes pancakes and blows up unicorn balloons.

One day, while Gru is out walking Kyle the pet, a strange woman approaches him.

"Mr. Gru? Hi! I'm Agent Lucy Wilde of the Anti-Villain League. You're gonna have to come with me."

Gru panics. "Oh, sorry...I, uh...FREEZE RAY!" he yells before grabbing his trusty Ray Gun and sending an icy blast at the stranger. Lucy deflects the attack with a Flamethrower.

"You really should announce your weapons *after* you fire them, Mr. Gru," Lucy says. "For example..." She pauses as she pulls something else out of her purse and suddenly fires at him. *ZAAAAAP!* "AVL-Issued Lipstick!" she cries.

The zapper knocks Gru out long enough for Lucy to drag him into her car and drive off.

Gru wakes up on a submarine, surrounded by strangers.

"My name is Silas Ramsbottom," says one of the men. "And we are the Anti-Villain League. If you rob a bank, we don't care, but if you steal the moon, we notice."

"First, you've got no proof I did that," says Gru. "Second, I put it back!"

Silas nods. "That's why we brought you here."

"Someone used a giant magnetic ship to steal a top secret formula called PX-41," Lucy explains.

She plays a video for Gru of a cute little bunny. When it nibbles a bit of PX-41, it turns into a big, furry, purple monster bunny!

"You usually don't see that in bunnies," Gru admits.

"Exactly! PX-41 is a dangerous weapon!" cries Lucy. "And we have found traces of it at the Paradise Mall."

"The mall?!" asks Gru in disbelief.

Silas jumps in. "We need you to go undercover and find it."

Gru gulps. "Um, okay, I guess."

Gru agrees to help the League.

The next day, he goes to the mall disguised as the owner of a cupcake shop called Bake My Day. He and a few Minions are decorating cupcakes when Lucy shows up.

"Hi, partner!" she says, startling Gru.

"What are you doing here?" demands Gru.

"Silas assigned me to work with you. Isn't this great?

Secret spy stuff! This is gonna be fun!" Lucy claps her hands
with excitement. "Come on, let's spy on the other stores and find
our suspect!"

A giant cupcake on the top of the store entrance has a camera
hidden in the cherry. Lucy and Gru have to stand uncomfortably
close together to be able to view the hidden video monitor.

"Our first suspect," says Lucy, "is Floyd Eaglesan. He owns the Eagle Hair Club."

Gru shakes his head. "There's no way that guy is a villain," he states. "His only crime is that wig!"

Lucy shrugs. "Our second suspect is Eduardo Perez, owner of Salsa & Salsa Restaurant. Uh-oh, and he's right here in the shop!"

They bump heads scrambling to greet Eduardo.

"*Buenos días*, my friends!" he says. "Welcome to the mall family! I am throwing a big Cinco de Mayo party, and I need two hundred cupcakes with the Mexican flag on them. I'll pick them up in a week. Okay, bye!"

After he leaves, Gru turns to Lucy. "That's him! He looks exactly like the villain El Macho, but twenty years older. El Macho was ruthless, dangerous, and as his name implies, very macho."

"Then I say we break in to his restaurant tonight after the mall closes to investigate," says Lucy. "It'll be my first break-in!"

That night, after the mall is closed, the two spies sneak back in. Gru is about to kick open the door to Eduardo's Salsa & Salsa Restaurant when Lucy stops him. She takes out her high-tech Nanobot Universal Key that can supposedly open any door. But when that fails to work, she gets frustrated and kicks the door open herself.

Once inside, they hear a clucking sound. They freeze, not wanting to be discovered. "What's that?" asks Lucy. Then a cute little chicken pops out from the kitchen.

But this is no normal chicken. It's a guard chicken!

It flies up to Gru and starts pecking at his bald head! "Get it off me! Get it off me!" cries Gru.

Lucy aims her AVL watch and squirts special foam all over the chicken. The gel quickly hardens into a ball, trapping the bird.

"BAWK!" it objects.

"What is wrong with that chicken?" asks Lucy. "That *pollo*? *Es loco*."

"There's the PX-41! In the safe! I know it!" Gru runs over to the safe and uses a fancy gadget to crack the code. Inside is a glass canister.

"I'm getting pretty good at this job!" he says as he grabs the canister.

"BAWK!" squawks the chicken.

"Someone's coming!" warns Lucy. "Let's go."

They cut a hole in the ceiling with a laser and get out just in time.

They hurry to the Anti-Villain League submarine and wake up Silas. "We found El Macho!" says Gru excitedly. "It's him. Look what we found in his restaurant's safe!"

Silas sticks a spoon in the canister and tastes it.

"No!" cries Gru. "Don't eat that. It's PX-41!"

"That is salsa," declares Silas. "Ripping good salsa at that. Tangy, but with a real kick."

"It's him," insists Gru. "What kind of person puts salsa in a safe? That's weird, right?"

"Mr. Gru, I do not appreciate my time being wasted on a wild-goose chase," scolds Silas. "I'm going back to bed."

"But there wasn't a goose—there was a chicken!" protests Gru.

When Gru delivers the cupcakes to the Cinco de Mayo
party, Eduardo greets him with a smile.

"*Mi compadre*, come have some guacamole with me!"
he says, leading Gru into an elevator. "I have something
planned for you."

During the long elevator ride deep underground,
Eduardo says, "I know who you are, Gru. And it's time
you know who I really am....I am El Macho."

"Oh! I knew it!" exclaims Gru.

They exit the elevator and enter a huge
underground lab.

"I acquired the most powerful substance on Earth with my magnetic ship!" explains El Macho. "How's that for macho? I'm going to use it to create a monster army of creatures that will eat entire cities…and we can do it together!" He claps Gru on the shoulder. "So, are you in?"

"Uh…yeah…probably…I mean, yes! Of course, yes. I just have a lot going on right now…but I am, like, ninety-seven percent in."

"You know what?" El Macho responds. "I am not so convinced that you are in. Let's make sure."

Just then, a rocket rises from steel doors in the ground. Attached to it are a shark, one hundred pounds of dynamite…and Lucy!

"Oh, hey, Gru! Turns out you were right about the whole El Macho thing, huh?" says Lucy.

Thinking fast, Gru grabs a weapon from his pocket and aims it at El Macho.

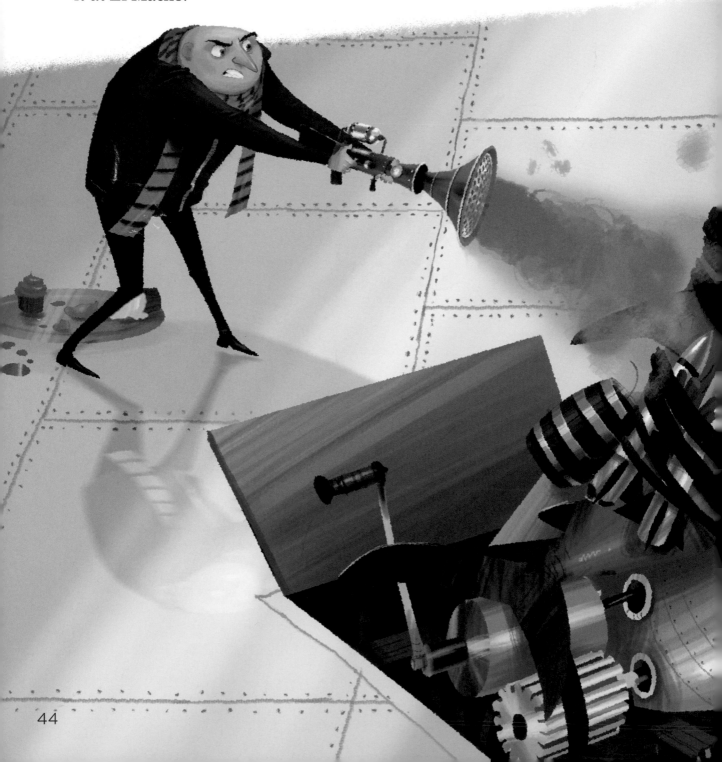

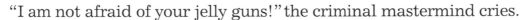

"I am not afraid of your jelly guns!" the criminal mastermind cries.

"Oh, this ain't no jelly gun, sunshine!" Gru retorts, pulling the trigger and releasing a horrible stinky fart.

The gas knocks El Macho right out! Gru leaps to Lucy's rescue.

Thanks to Gru and his new friends at the Anti-Villain League, El Macho is behind bars and the PX-41 is far from anyone who can misuse it. The world is safe from harm…for now.

ATTACK OF THE EVIL MINIONS!

By Kirsten Mayer • Illustrated by Ed Miller

Based on the Motion Picture Screenplay
Written by Cinco Paul & Ken Daurio

See that guy there among all the yellow fellows? That's Gru. He was once a villain, but now he has turned the secret lab under his house into a jelly factory! The yellow fellows are Minions. See all the Minions at work making jelly? Well, most of them are working.

Quiet, please—
testing in progress.

The bad news is that the jelly tastes gross.
Kevin asks Gru, "Boss! Topah-leena-la belly?"
Gru throws his hands up in the air.
"You know what?" he says. "Let's shut it down. We are officially out of the jelly business!"

The Minions cheer! Then they smash all the jelly jars to celebrate.

SPLAT!
SPLAT!
SPLAT!
SPLAT!
SPLAT!

Later that night, the doorbell rings at Gru's house. . . .

DING-DONG!

"Bello?"

Oh no! A mysterious villain grabs the Minion! So many Minions, so little time.

Meanwhile, the other Minions are hanging out. It's good to be a Minion!

"Hey! Jerry, Kevin, keep an eye on things, okay?" asks Gru. "I'm going out."

The Minions take a look around the house. All is quiet, so they decide to have some fun.

Kevin nudges Jerry. "Hey, putt-putt?" he asks.

Jerry giggles. "Oh! Ha, ha, ha!"

"Una,
doo..."

CLANG!

They hear a loud
noise outside!

The Minions tiptoe outside, looking for a burglar.
"Boca? Boca?" they wonder.

Suddenly, a stray cat jumps out of a garbage can.

CLANG!

Kevin and Jerry laugh at each other for being so scared.

"Looka, too!"
They point at each other.

The pointing turns into a wrestling match, but they freeze when a strange beam of light shines down from above. . . .

Two more Minions missing!

The next day, an ice cream truck drives by the house!

RING-A-LING!

Gru should really mind his Minions—
someone keeps taking them!

Someone has collected mucho
Minions and put them on a beach.
They don't know it, but the Minions are
trapped! What will happen to them?
A Minion is a terrible thing to waste.

"Bello!" says Kevin.

"Compai!" says Tom.

In another secret lab, the villain has plans
for the Minions! The Minions don't notice the
purple goo.
What will that purple goo do to them?

"BLAAAH..."

It turns Tom into a monster!
Yellow is no longer mellow.

"BLAAARGH!"

But one Evil Minion
is never enough.

The new Evil Minions are
unstoppable.

Flames don't burn them. Explosives
are just a mild tummy ache. And they
eat metal...lots of metal.

The mastermind behind the Minion mania is known as El Macho!

"The time has come, my purple army!" he cries. "I will unleash you, and you will eat the entire city! The world will be ours!"

El Macho looks around. "Hey! Minions, what are you doing? Pay attention! Stop eating the rocket! We need that! Get a hold of your brains! Everybody, back in line!"

El Macho unleashes his Evil Minions onto the world.
First stop: Gru's house. It's an attack of the Evil Minions!

Purple Evil Minions eat through
the walls of Gru's lab! The Minions
don't know what to do!
What should they do?

One Minion throws a leftover jar of jelly at the purple monsters.

The jelly is a cure!
The monster turns
back into Kevin!

"GULP!"

Gru assembles his Minions—now he knows what to do. He points to a vat of unused jelly and says, "Team Minion, all hands on deck! Let's put this horrible jelly to good use!"

"*Eye, eye*, captain!" they shout.

The Minions load globs of jelly onto a blaster ship and zoom into the air to zap all the Evil Minions with splats of sticky stuff.

"It's over, El Macho! You lose!" yells Gru in triumph as Minions swarm the villain.

"Noooooo!" cries El Macho. "My Minions!"

"*My* Minions," says Gru. "The best Minions ever!"

MINIONS

Dracula's Last Birthday

By Lucy Rosen
Illustrated by Ed Miller

Minions have roamed the earth since the beginning of time. Before there was Gru, before there were evil gadgets to invent, before there were super villains who wanted to take over the world…there were Minions.

Ever since the very first Minion crawled out of the ocean and onto dry land, these little yellow creatures have been searching for one thing: the most terrible, wicked, despicable master they could find.

The Minions lived to serve.
They had no trouble tracking
down the biggest, baddest
dinosaur…

…or helping a wicked pharaoh
erect a pyramid.

But even though they just wanted to help, something always went wrong.

Whenever disaster struck, the Minions kept moving. One day, they came across a dark stone castle. It looked creepy, creaky, and cold. It was perfect! The Minions couldn't wait to meet whoever lived there.

The Minions pushed open the front door and peeked inside. Out of nowhere, bats came flying toward them!

"Oh, la no! Stopa, stopa!" they cried, trying to get away from the bat attack. The Minions tumbled into dusty cobwebs. They jumped into sticky cauldrons. They hid behind heavy, dirty curtains.

When the bats finally left, the Minions came out of their hiding spots and looked around. At the end of the long, dark hallway was a spooky wooden coffin. "Oooooh," they said.

One of the Minions walked up to the coffin. He knocked on the lid. It burst wide open. Dracula was inside!

"Velcome to my castle!" the evil vampire bellowed.

"Si, si, si!" cried the Minions. They couldn't believe it. They had found their new master!

"Big boss! Big boss! Big boss!" they cheered.

The Minions got right to work trying to help Dracula however they could. First, they decided to clean up the castle. Carl and Mike took turns sweeping the cobwebs.

"Me do it," Carl said.

"No, me, me do it," Mike replied.

"Speta, me la do it," Carl insisted.

"Me!" said Mike.

"Me!" said Carl.

Soon enough, the two Minions were tussling down the hallway. They bounced and rolled and rumbled all around, until they got tangled up in an enormous web!

Next, the Minions replaced all of Dracula's melted candles. One by one, they removed the old wax. They carefully polished each candlestick. They gently put in fresh new candles.

Then they lit them all with a torch.

Finally, at the end of every day, the Minions helped
Dracula get ready to go to sleep. They hung up his
cape, fluffed his itchy pillow, and reminded him to
always brush his fangs before bedtime.

"Scusa, big boss? Floss-floss?" they said.

Over time, Dracula came to rely on the Minions and think of them as his friends. He even let them in on a secret.

"Tomorrow vill be my three-hundred-und-fifty-seventh birthday!" he said proudly.

The Minions were excited. They wanted to throw their evil boss an evil party to celebrate his many years of evildoing. But they didn't have much time.

Kevin made a list of all the things they'd need to do: Bake a cake. Make drinks. Find a great gift…

Dave and Paul got started on the cake. They mixed together eggs, flour, strawberries, and sugar. "Yum, yum," they said.

Chuck and Norbert made punch in one of Dracula's cauldrons. They put ice cream and fresh fruit in the juice. Delicious!

Finding the right gift was the hardest part. What does a Minion get for the villain who has it all? The Minions put their heads together until they thought of the perfect present: a portrait of Dracula with all his yellow friends by his side.

They got to work painting their masterpiece.

Happy Birthday

357

Finally, it was time! The big day had arrived. Dave and Paul led Dracula to the ballroom, where the party was just getting started.

"Surprise!" the Minions yelled.

"Ah, how vonderful!" Dracula cackled as he sipped from his goblet of fruit punch.

"Big boss, big cake," said Kevin. He opened the door to reveal Minions carrying a strawberries-and-cream cake.

Dracula took a deep breath and blew out the candles.

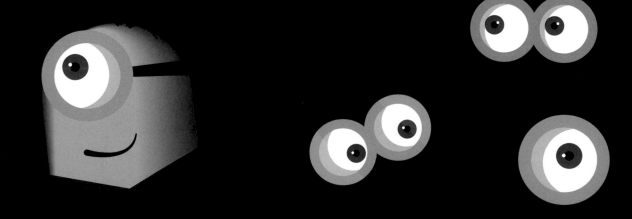

They were about to give Dracula his present when Norbert realized it was too dark to see. They had gone to a lot of trouble making it perfect, and he wanted to make sure their boss would enjoy it.

"Le idea!" Kevin said.

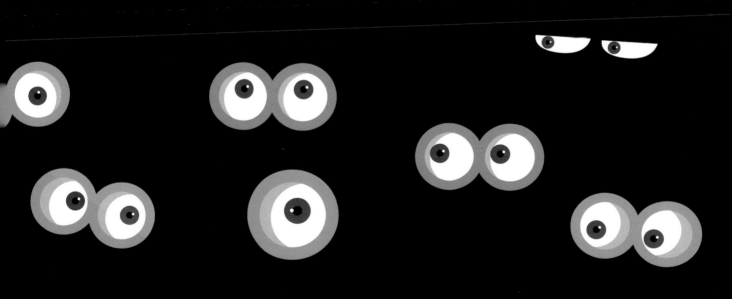

The Minions grabbed the curtains and pulled them apart. Sunlight poured in and onto their painting.

"Paratu, big boss!" the Minions cooed, admiring their work of art.

Dracula didn't reply.

"Big boss?" they said.

Dracula did not say a word.

The Minions turned around.

Where Dracula had been sitting, there was now a big pile of ashes. The Minions forgot about the vampire's biggest weakness: sunlight!

"Uh, no," said Stuart, slapping his forehead. "Not again."

Another evil boss, another Minion accident. The little yellow creatures sighed and moved on.

Soon, they found another perfect despicable master in a French captain. At least—that is—until they messed up again.

OOPS!

MINIONS PARADISE™

PHIL SAVES THE DAY!

Adapted by Trey King • Illustrated by Ed Miller

Based on the Minions Paradise video game

It's been a long time since the Minions had a vacation.

This year, the whole tribe decided on a tropical cruise for their vacation. As they sail the seven seas, there are all kinds of fun activities—and things to eat. The buffet is filled with recipes featuring the Minions' favorite foods: banana splits, banana pudding, banana bread, banana cake…they have it all!

The Minions each have something to share.

Charlie is making balloon animals!

Barry makes his famous burritos.

Amazing chef Ken makes
a delicious banana cake!

And then there's Phil...

Phil has a habit of messing things up. While hula dancing, Phil accidentally knocks over Ken's delicious cake, ruining it for his buddies.

Everyone walks away upset at Phil.
No one likes dirty floor cake. Poor Phil.

Phil tries to think of a way to make it up to the other Minions.

He makes balloon animals— but they keep popping!

He makes burritos— but they're way too spicy!

He even tries to make a cake— but he burns it beyond recognition.

Phil decides some harmless sunbathing might be a good way to spend the rest of his day.

But a well-oiled Minion makes things a little slippery....Phil better hold on to something. Oops! Too late!

Phil is as slippery as a bar of soap! As he slides
all over the ship, he makes a real mess of things.

When he hits the captain's wheel, Phil knocks the ship off course!
Hold on, everybody!

The ship crashes into a large rock, causing water to start pouring in.

Ahhhh!

Phil flies off the ship and skips across the water like a stone. He lands on a deserted island. Phil's really done it this time!

Uh-oh! The ship is sinking, and all the Minions are making a swim for it. They do *not* look happy.

What is Phil going to do?!

Phil has ruined the other Minions' vacation.
Boy, are they mad! He'd better hurry!

A coconut falls from above and hits
Phil in the head. This gives him an idea!

BOINK!

Phil makes a tiki lounge! He also makes welcome baskets for everyone. And he makes lots of smoothies!

Everyone gets a banana drink from the smoothie bar! Suddenly, being trapped on a deserted island doesn't seem so bad. Good job, Phil!

Now the whole tribe is on an island and having the time of their lives. There are games for everyone and a pool with water slides. But the best part of all…is the amazing food! Who wants more banana smoothies?

So perhaps Phil *doesn't* ruin everything—he makes it better! He's turned a disaster into a party! Well done, Phil!

Mower Minions

DESPICABLE ME — MINION MADE

Adapted by Trey King • Illustrated by Ed Miller

(Based on *Mowers Minions* short, original Script by Glenn McCoy & Dave Rosenbaum)

What are the Minions doing on a lazy afternoon?
Watching TV, of course!

An amazing commercial comes on. It's an ad for Barb's Blender—
great for making banana smoothies! The Minions *have* to have it!

How will the Minions get inside their piggy bank? They could use dynamite! (Or just a hammer.)

Inside, they find a quarter.
That's not enough to buy
the new blender!

Outside their window, they see Mrs. Rose paying Larry for cleaning up her yard. That gives the Minions a great idea!

The Minions borrow a lawn mower and some lawn tools from Larry. He won't mind, right? Now they just need to find their first customers.

Some residents sit on the front porch of a local retirement home. The Minions offer their new lawn services.

The residents are a little hard of hearing, but nonetheless, they hire the Minions to work on the yard. Time to get to work, Minions!

Dave takes charge and hops on the lawn mower.
How difficult can it be to drive one of those things?
It turns out...*very* hard. The mower is out of control!

VROOM

On the other side of the yard, Jerry rakes leaves when he bumps into a gnome.

Instantly, the two become locked in a staring contest!

The Minions are working hard…or are they hardly working?

Watch where you step, Dave. *Oops!* Too late.

Time for yard cleanup!

Uh-oh! Looks like the leafblower is blowing up someone's hazmat suit!

RRRRR

One Minion is running around with a beehive on his head.
Another turns green when he smells something yucky.
Another Minion is bouncing around the yard in a blown-up suit.
Another crashes the mower.
And another blows up the barbeque grill!

The Minions feel terrible. They were trying to do an honest day's work to earn money, but everything went wrong.

They go to the porch to apologize
to the residents of the home.

The people are laughing so hard, they can barely stand. "Thank you so much for that," says Gertrude. "That's the most we've laughed in a very long time."

"Here you go, young man," adds Gertrude. "Payment for a really funny show. Spend it wisely."

They did it! The Minions can
buy their blender now! Hooray!

I ♥ DISCO

Bzzz

After a few days of using the blender nonstop to make banana smoothies, the Minions can barely move! They're *sooooo* full.

Wait! A new-and-*improved* blender? With an arm that peels the bananas for you? The Minions have to have it! Where are they going to get the money?

It's time for the Minions to get a *another* job!

EXPLODING MINIONS

A CARD GAME
FOR PEOPLE WHO ARE INTO
BANANAS AND EXPLOSIONS
AND FLAMING UNICORNS
AND SOMETIMES FIRE HYDRANTS.

AGES 7+
2-5 PLAYERS

A GAME BY
EXPLODING KITTENS

EXPLODING MINIONS

A CARD GAME
FOR PEOPLE WHO ARE INTO
BANANAS AND EXPLOSIONS
AND FLAMING UNICORNS
AND SOMETIMES FIRE HYDRANTS.

  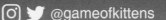